Ottoline at Sea

Chris Riddell is an accomplished artist and political cartoonist for the *Observer*. His books have won many awards, including the Kate Greenaway Medal, the Nestlé Children's Book Prize and the Red House Children's Book Award. *Goth Girl and the Ghost of a Mouse* won the Costa Children's Book Award in 2013.

Also available

Ottoline and the Yellow Cat
Ottoline Goes to School

Goth Girl and the Ghost of a Mouse
Goth Girl and the Fete Worse Than Death

panmacmillan.com/ChrisRiddell

Praise for the Ottoline books

'Beautifully illustrated' *Guardian*

'Each page is designed with retro elegance'
Sunday Times

'Delightfully elegant, packed with quirky detail, clever pictoral surprises and visual jokes'
Daily Mail

'Possibly the most instantly covetable book ever published' *Sunday Telegraph*

Chris RIDDELL

Ottoline at Sea

MACMILLAN CHILDREN'S BOOKS

For my nephew, Stephen

Chapter One

Ottoline lived on the twenty-fourth floor of the Pepperpot Building. It was on 3rd Street, which had Gruberman's Korean Theatre at one end and Pettigrew Park and Ornamental Gardens at the other. In the middle was the 3rd Street Shoe Store.

Ottoline lived in Apartment 243 with Mr. Munroe, who was small and hairy and didn't like the rain or having his hair brushed.

Ottoline and Mr. Munroe were good at solving tricky problems and working out clever plans, which they did quite a lot . . .

Like the time they caught the notorious jewel thief the Yellow Cat . . .

. . . and the time they came face to face with the ghost of the Horse of the Hammersteins.

But whatever Ottoline and Mr. Munroe did, they did it together.

STARGAZERS
GIGGLE GLASSES
DR. J.T. ECKLEBERG'S "BOG GOGGLES"
EMPERORS' HATS
OTTOLINE'S PARENTS WERE ROVING COLLECTORS WHO TRAVELLED THE WORLD COLLECTING THINGS. THEY WERE AWAY A LOT BUT MADE SURE OTTOLINE WAS WELL LOOKED AFTER, AND KEPT IN TOUCH WITH POSTCARDS WHICH OTTOLINE KEPT IN HER POSTCARD COLLECTION
METEORITES
BLUE BOTTLES
OLINE COLLECTED SHOES. WHENEVER BOUGHT A PAIR WOULD WEAR ONE PUT THE OTHER IN DD SHOE COLLECTION
SNUFF BOTTLES
HOT-WATER BOTTLES
MR. MUNROE COLLECTED ODD BITS OF STRING WHICH HE ADDED TO THE BALL OF STRING IN HIS BEDROOM
3 STREET SHOES

6

One morning at the beginning of the school holidays . . .

That afternoon Ottoline and and Mr. Munroe were walking down 3rd Street when a large billboard caught Mr. Munroe's eye. He stopped and pointed.

"Not now, Mr. Munroe," said Ottoline absent-mindedly. "When we go on holiday I'm going to need some shoes . . ."

"*Bonjour,* Ottoline!" said Vivienne of the 3rd Street Shoe Store. "I see you've spotted the Penguin Slippers. I also have your size in the Eskimo Pumps, the Caribou Platforms and a pair of quite unusual Moose Boots."

"I'll take them all," said Ottoline. "You can't have too many shoes on holiday. Could you tie them in a parcel with lots of string, please?"

That evening Ottoline and Mr. Munroe sat down to dinner. Ottoline had macaroni cheese and lime-juice cordial, freshly delivered to the table by the Home-Cooked Meal Company. Mr. Munroe had a bowl of porridge and a mug of hot chocolate, which is what he always had.

Mr. Munroe was just about to sip his hot chocolate when . . .

. . . he noticed something rather unusual. He rushed down to Ottoline's end of the table.

"Don't make a mess, Mr. Munroe," said Ottoline distractedly. She was busy rereading her favourite book, *The Whistle of the Wild – Tales of Animal Hitchhiking* by Thør Thørenssen, to get some ideas for where to go on holiday. She had just got to the bit about being polite to llamas.

The following morning Max the paper boy delivered the *Big City Enquirer* to Apartment 243. Ottoline was reading the postcard that she'd just found on the welcome mat.

"Going somewhere nice for the holidays?" he asked.

THIS IS THE POSTCARD

"I haven't decided," said Ottoline. She began flicking through the newspaper. "Yet."

POSTCARD

Dearest O,

Pa and I are troll spotting and Pa thought he'd found the footprints of "Quite Big Foot" but they turned out to belong to a dancing elk!

lots of love,

Ma.

P.S. You and Mr. Monroe should have a holiday. We are sending a parcel.

For the rest of the day Mr. Munroe kept seeing strange and unusual things.

Nobody else did. They were all too busy . . .

Mr. Munroe felt sad.

But Ottoline didn't notice.

Chapter Two

"Just going down to do the laundry!" called Ottoline later that evening. Mr. Munroe didn't hear her.

In the basement a large bear was sorting through a pile of clothes.

"Hello," Ottoline said. "You are just the bear to talk to. I am thinking of taking Mr. Munroe on holiday. He could do with a change of scene."

"What a good idea," said the bear. "Anywhere nice?"

"Somewhere hot and sunny," said Ottoline. "Mr. Munroe doesn't like getting cold or wet."

She picked up a basket of clean laundry. "Have you seen my stripy socks?"

Mr. Munroe climbed to the top of the fire escape and on to the roof of the Pepperpot Building, which is where he always went when he needed to be alone. Except that evening he didn't stop there . . .

Mr. Munroe carried on up the dome of the pepperpot . . .

. . . right to the very top, higher than he'd ever climbed before.

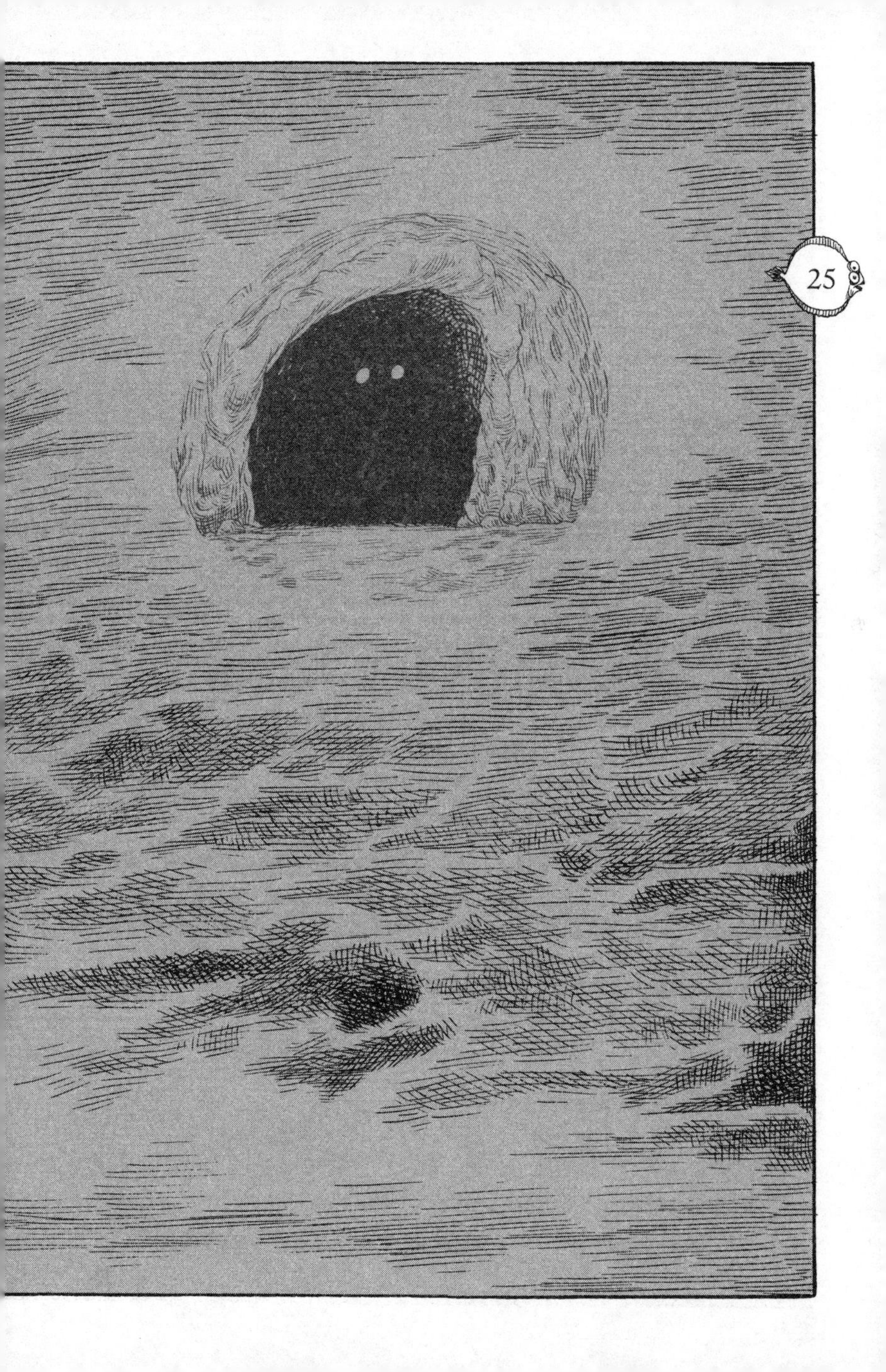

“Pahang is very sunny at this time of year,” the bear said, passing Ottoline a handkerchief.

"I could visit my friend the Sultana," said Ottoline. "She has a hairy elephant called Bye-Bye."

"Sounds lovely," said the bear. "I could help you pack." He folded a pair of polka-dot knickerbockers. "Will you be eavesdropping this evening?"

"Only for a little bit," said Ottoline.

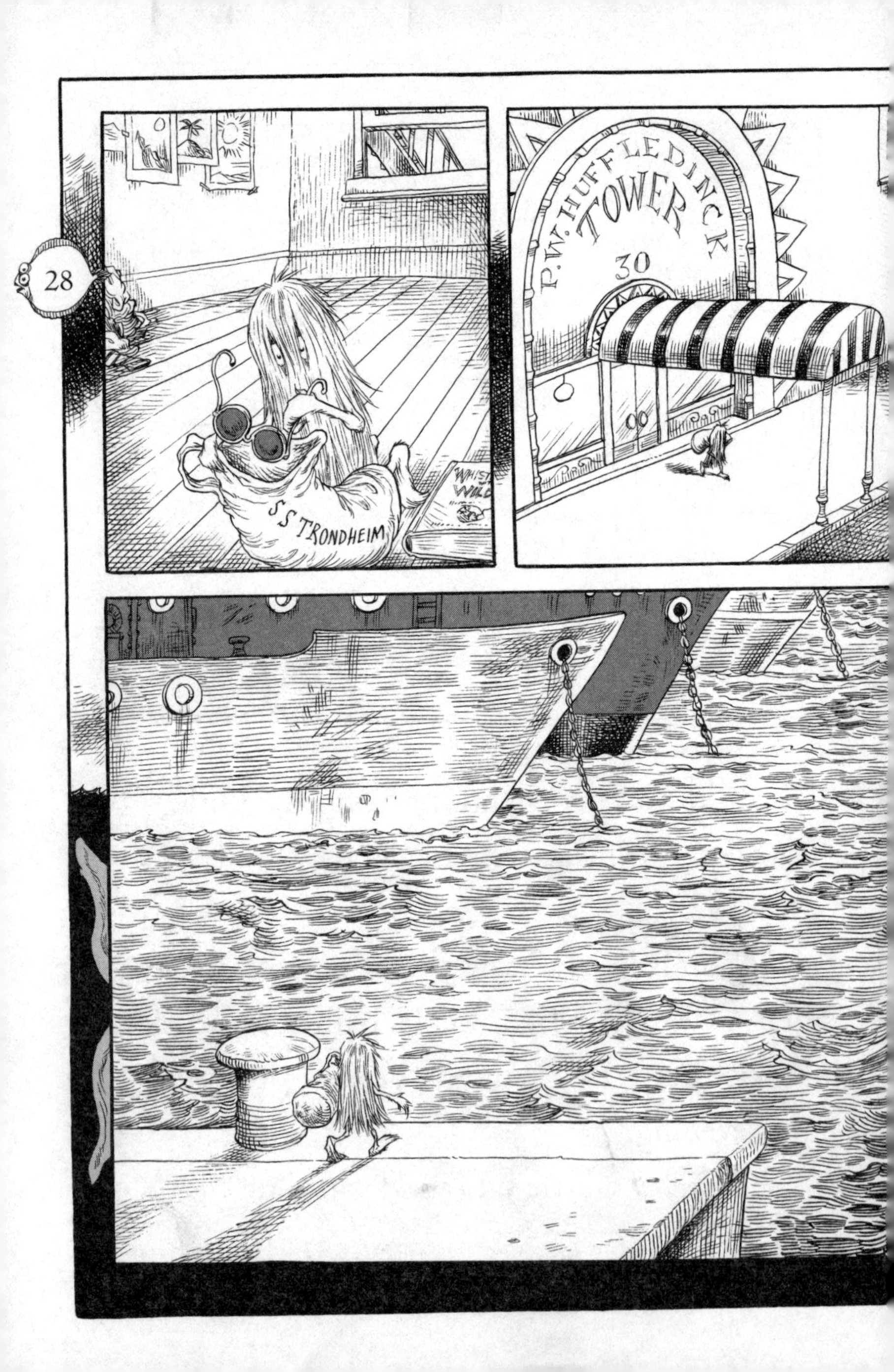
S S TRONDHEIM
P.W. HUFFLEDINCK
TOWER
30

S.S TRONDHEIM

Ottoline and the bear went back up to Apartment 243.

"Mr. Munroe!" called Ottoline excitedly, knocking on the door to his room. "I know the perfect place to go on holiday! The bear has come to help us pack and . . ." She stopped.

Mr. Munroe's room was empty.

“Where is he?” asked Ottoline with tears in her eyes. “It’s not like Mr. Munroe to go anywhere without telling me. And look! He’s taken his duffel bag . . .”

She began to cry.

Just then Mrs. Pasternak and her pet monkey, Morris, from Apartment 244 came in. “The front door was open, Ottoline, dear,” she said. “Is everything all right?”

"No!" sobbed Ottoline. "Mr. Munroe has disappeared and I don't know where he is."

"I think I do," said Mrs. Pasternak.

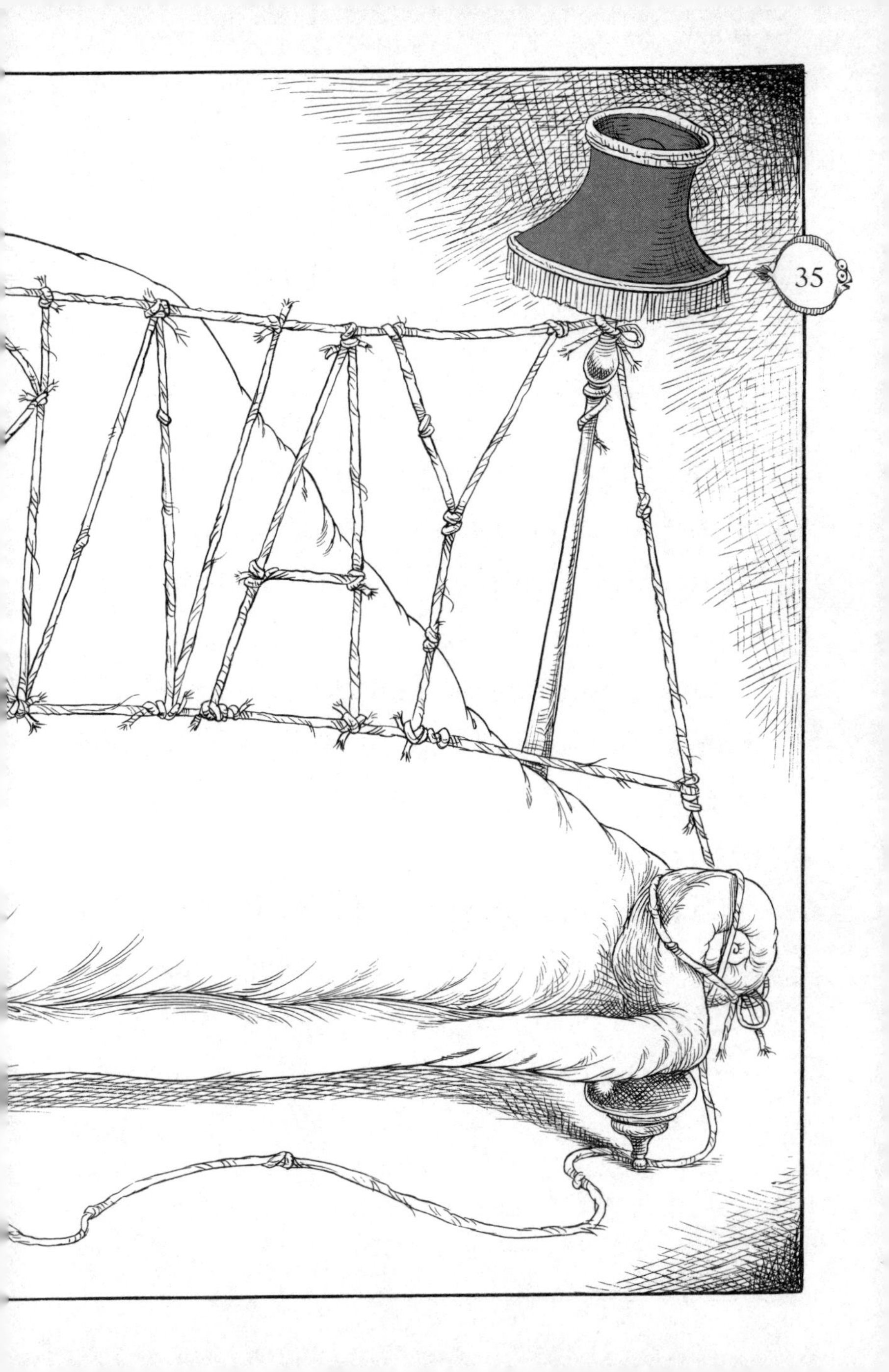

Chapter Three

"Mr. Munroe was obviously trying to tell you something, dear," Mrs. Pasternak said as she poured them all another cup of tea from the four-spouted teapot.

"Yes. It must be my fault Mr. Munroe has gone to Norway all by himself," said Ottoline tearfully. The bear offered her a large spotted handkerchief.

"There, there, dear," said Mrs. Pasternak sympathetically. "Worse things happen at sea. What you need is a good night's sleep. I'm sure things will seem better in the morning."

But that night Ottoline couldn't sleep.

She lay wide awake, thinking about Mr. Munroe . . .

. . . and missing him.

In the morning Ottoline found a postcard and a brown-paper parcel on the doormat.

THESE WERE INSIDE
ROVING COLLECTORS'
TRAVEL PASS
PERMITS Ottoline Brown
AND ASSISTANT TO ROVE FOR 17 DAYS ONLY

41

LOOK THROUGH HERE
PRESS THIS BUTTON
ROVE O'MATIC
TRAVEL CAMERA
PHOTOGRAPH COMES OUT HERE

Ottoline rushed to the cupboard where the bear liked to sleep.

"Wake up!" she said. "I'm going to Norway to find Mr. Munroe! Will you come as my assistant?"

"I'd be delighted," said the bear.

THIS IS WHAT THE BEAR PACKED
TAGONIAN ONCHO
HIMALAYAN RAINHOOD
SUITCASE CONTAINING HAIRBRUSH AND CANADIAN SOCKS
TRIPLE-BOBBLE HAT
NOTEBOOK
TRAVEL PASS
ROVE O'MATIC CAMERA
MOOSE BOOT
CARIBOU PLATFORM SHOE

Ottoline knocked on the door of Apartment 244. "Good morning, Mrs. Pasternak!" she said. "You were right, things do seem better. We're going to Norway to find Mr. Munroe! Could you give us a lift to Big City Harbour?"

"Oh, I think I can do better than that," said Mrs. Pasternak mysteriously.

Ten minutes later they were driving down 3rd Street in Mrs. Pasternak's Warren-Harding Continental. The automobile was so big that Mrs. Pasternak couldn't see over the steering wheel and had to look through it instead. Morris the monkey stuck his head out of the window and gave hand signals.

THE EMPRESS TINA
THE MARJORIE

Mrs. Pasternak drove past all the ships that were moored, right the way to the very end of the dock, until Morris waved STOP!

Mrs. Pasternak walked down to the edge of the dock and peered into Big City Harbour's murky waters.

"Cooo-eeee! Jules!" she called. "It's Aunt Judy. I hope this isn't an inconvenient time . . ."

A moment later a tall periscope appeared.

Mrs. Pasternak waved. "Sorry to bother you, dear," she said.

The periscope disappeared back into the water, which began to swirl and bubble . . .

. . . and a small, slightly rusty-looking green submarine rose to the surface. A hatch opened and four heads appeared.

"This is my nephew, Captain Jules Pasternak," said Mrs. Pasternak proudly, "and his crew: Derek, Phoebe and Nugent."

"Hello, Aunt Judy," said Captain Pasternak. "What can I do for you?"

THE
IRON
Leviathan

“My next-door neighbour, Ottoline Brown, and her assistant want to go to Norway,” Mrs. Pasternak explained. “Can you help, Jules, dear?”

“An Amateur Roving Collector, eh?” said Captain Pasternak, looking at Ottoline’s travel pass and stroking his beard thoughtfully. “I have a few errands to run and some underwater exploring to do, but I can take you some of the way,” he said. “And with your travel pass you should be able to pick up another lift.”

“Thank you,” said Ottoline, climbing aboard.

"Take care," called Mrs. Pasternak from the dock, waving an embroidered handkerchief, "and remember to wear a vest!"

"Aye aye!" called Ottoline as the *Iron Leviathan* headed out to sea.

"Batten down the hatches," ordered Captain Pasternak in a cheerful voice, "and prepare to dive!"

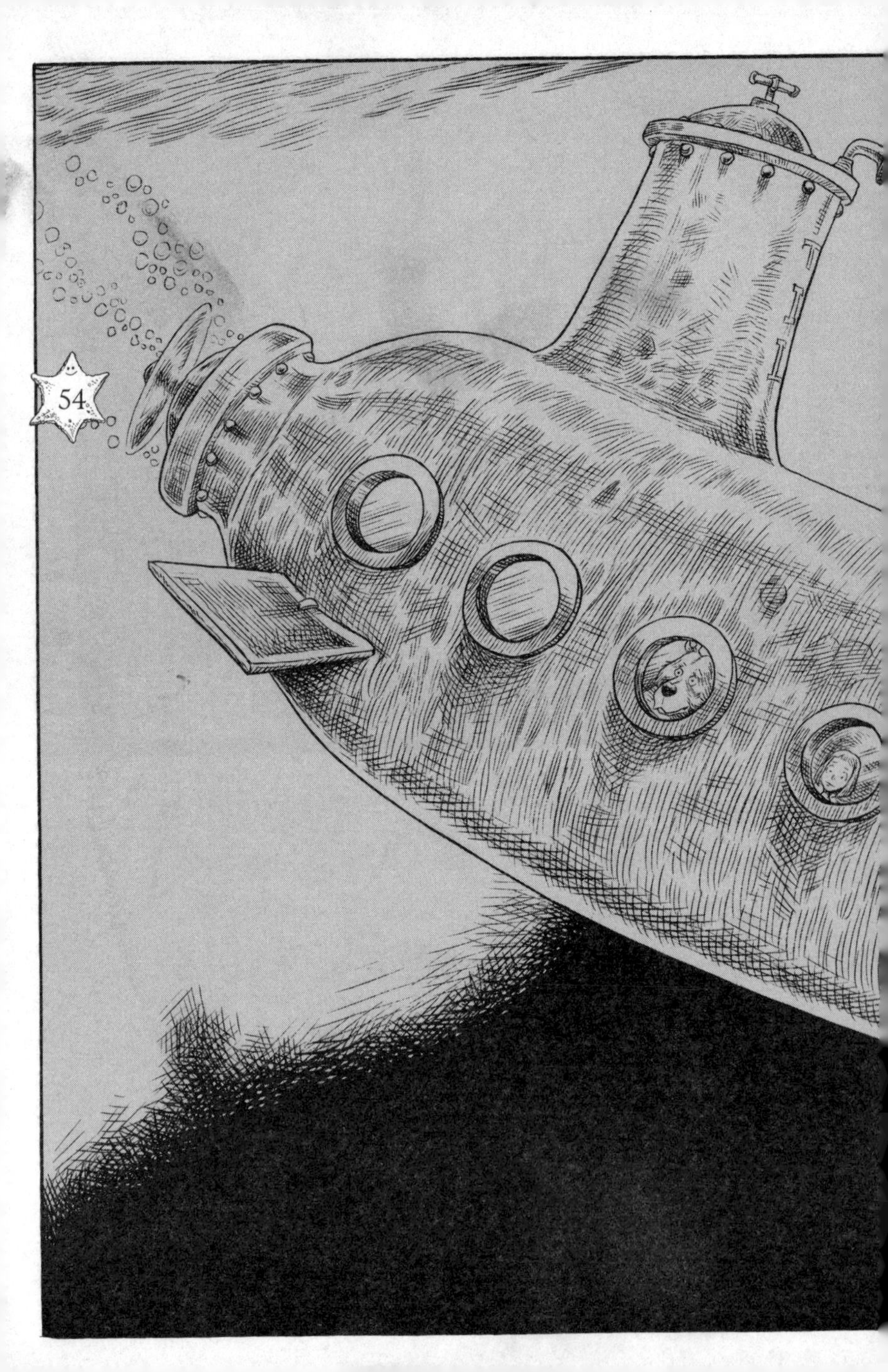

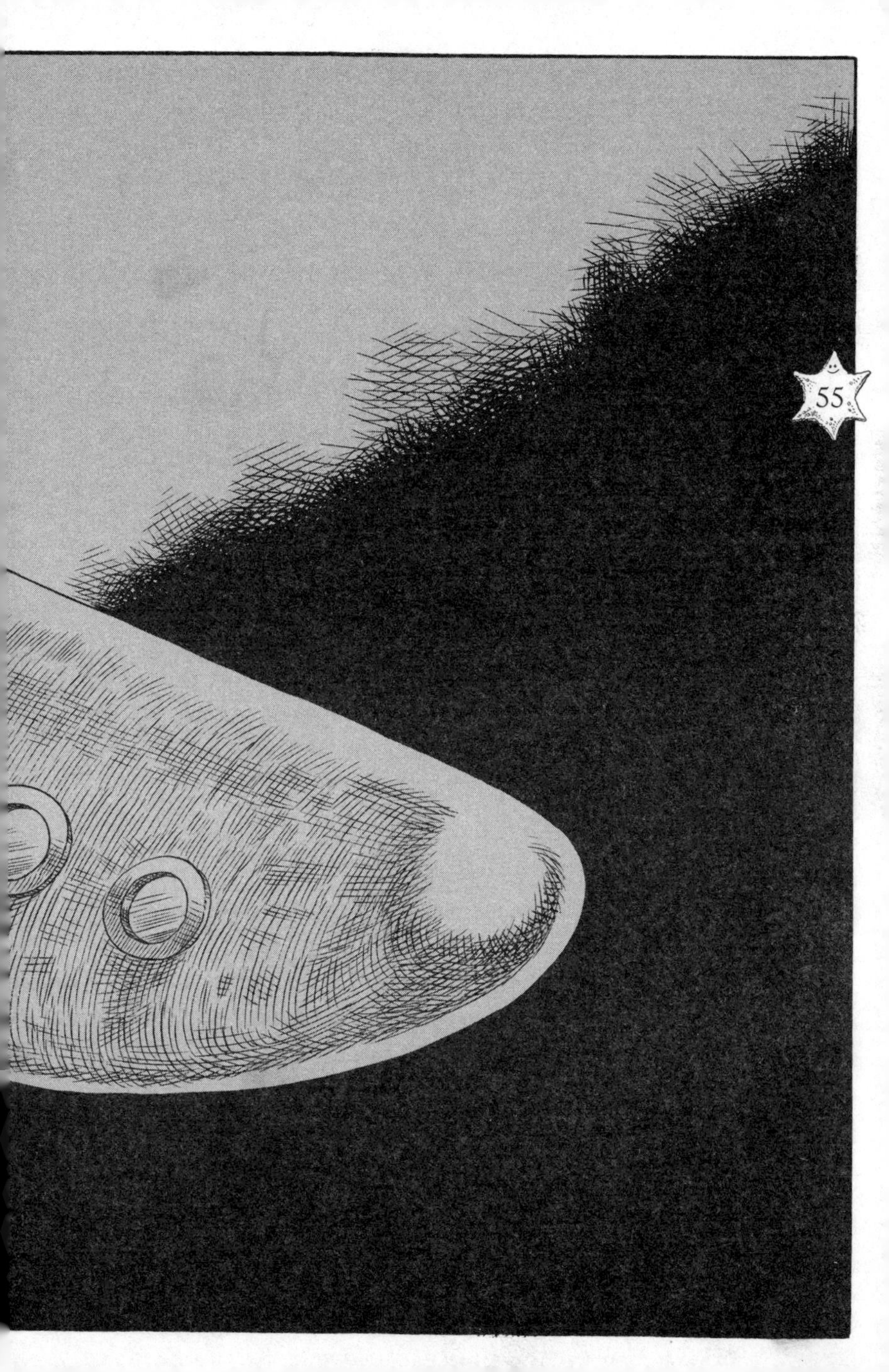

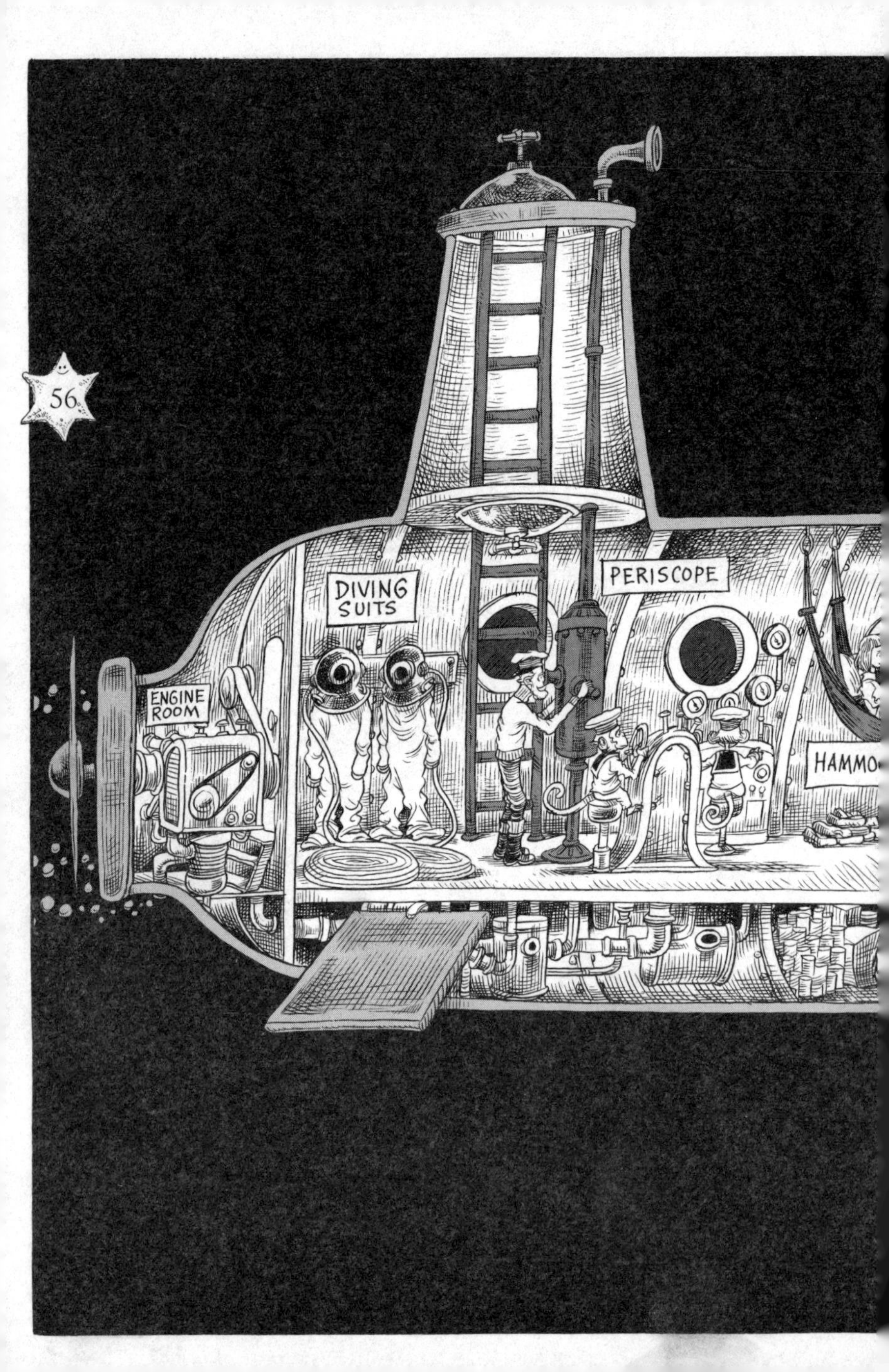
ENGINE ROOM
DIVING SUITS
PERISCOPE

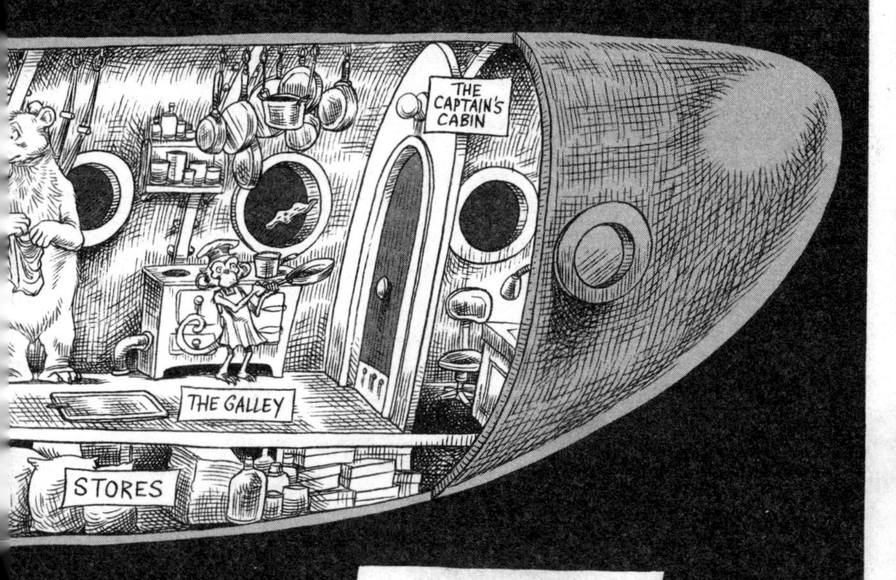
THE CAPTAIN'S CABIN
THE GALLEY
STORES
THE IRON LEVIATHAN

Ottoline and the bear got settled into their hammocks as the *Iron Leviathan* went deeper and deeper under the sea.

"I miss Mr. Munroe," said Ottoline sadly.

"I know it won't be the same," said the bear, "but I packed a hairbrush . . ."

"Why Norway of all places?" Ottoline mumbled to herself as she brushed the bear's fur. "Mr. Munroe doesn't like the cold and rain . . ."

"Ah! Unless, of course, he wants to help Ma and Pa look for Quite Big Foot . . ."

"Quite Big Foot the Abominable Troll?!" exclaimed Captain Pasternak.

"Terrifying creature, by all accounts. Eight foot tall, and with a temper to match! But very hard to find, a little like mermaids . . ."

"Mermaids?" said Ottoline.

"Yes," said Captain Pasternak. "Would you care to take a look?"

"Yes, please," said Ottoline. She looked through the periscope.

"I can't see any mermaids," said Ottoline.

"Exactly," said Captain Pasternak, taking a deep-sea diving suit off a hook. "Time for a closer inspection."

Chapter Four

SS TRONDHEIM

SS TRONDHEIM

SS TRONDHEIM

SS TRONDHEI

SSTRONDHEIM

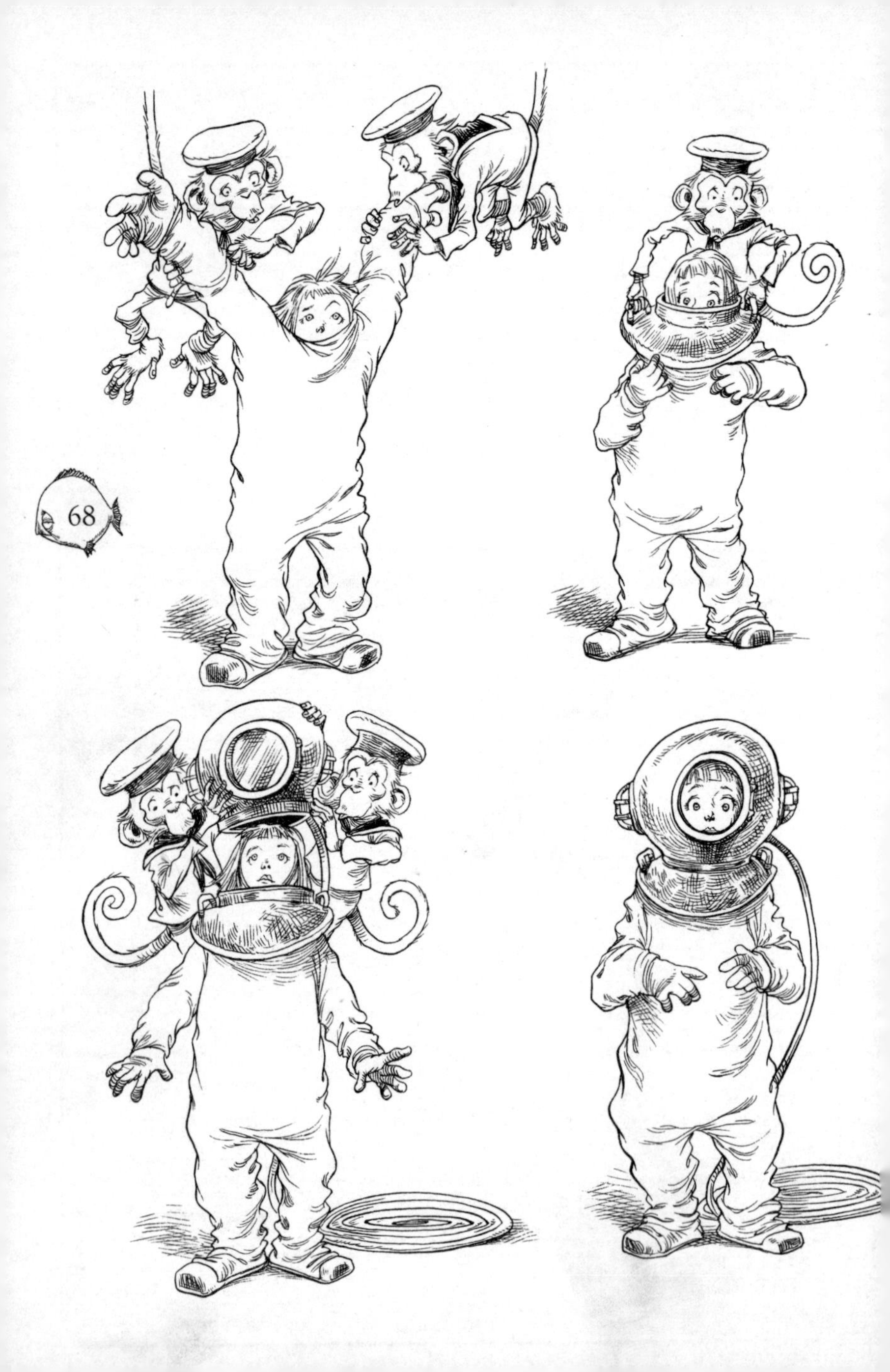

On-board the *Iron Leviathan,* Derek, Phoebe and Nugent helped Ottoline into a deep-sea diving suit.

"It really suits you," said the bear.

"Ready to look for mermaids?" said Captain Pasternak in a rather muffled voice.

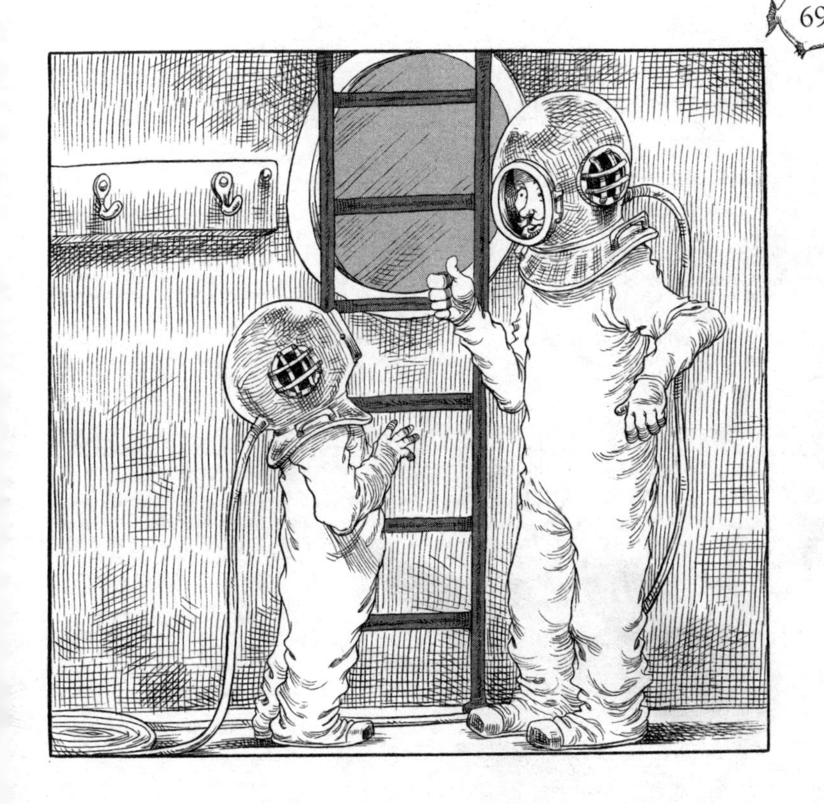

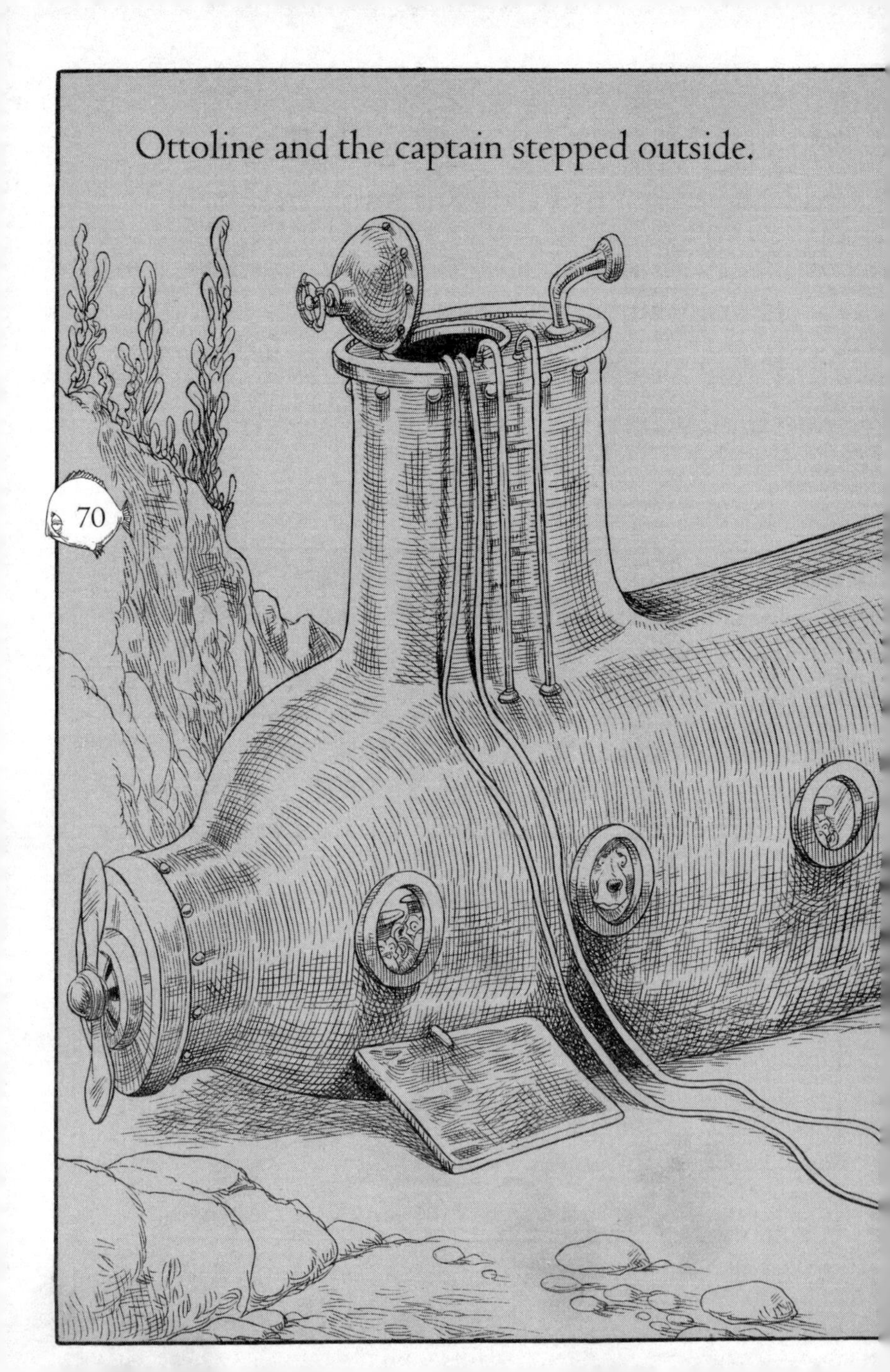

Ottoline and the captain stepped outside.

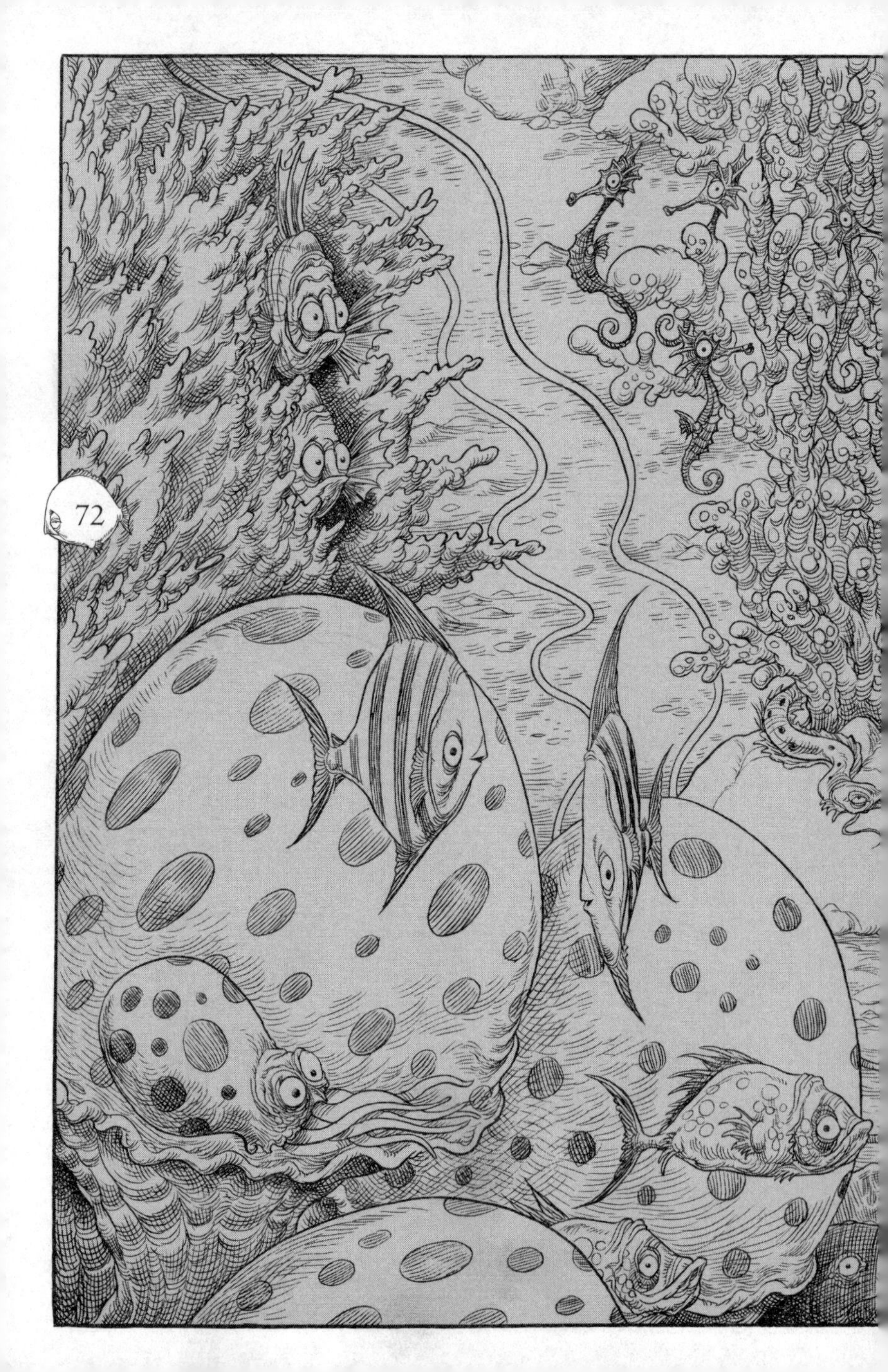

WELCOME

74

Ottoline thought she'd caught a glimpse of something interesting and wanted to investigate, but they had reached the limit of their oxygen pipes and couldn't go any further. So they turned round and went back to the *Iron Leviathan*.

"No mermaids today," said Captain Pasternak in a gurgling underwater voice. "Underwater exploration is like that – you never know what's around the next corner."

Chapter Five

SS TRONDHEIM

SSTRONDHEIM

Ottoline was making some Amateur Roving Collectors' notes in her notebook, when there was a tap-tap-tapping sound at the porthole.

Ottoline looked up. Quickly she grabbed the Rove O'Matic travel camera and started taking photographs.

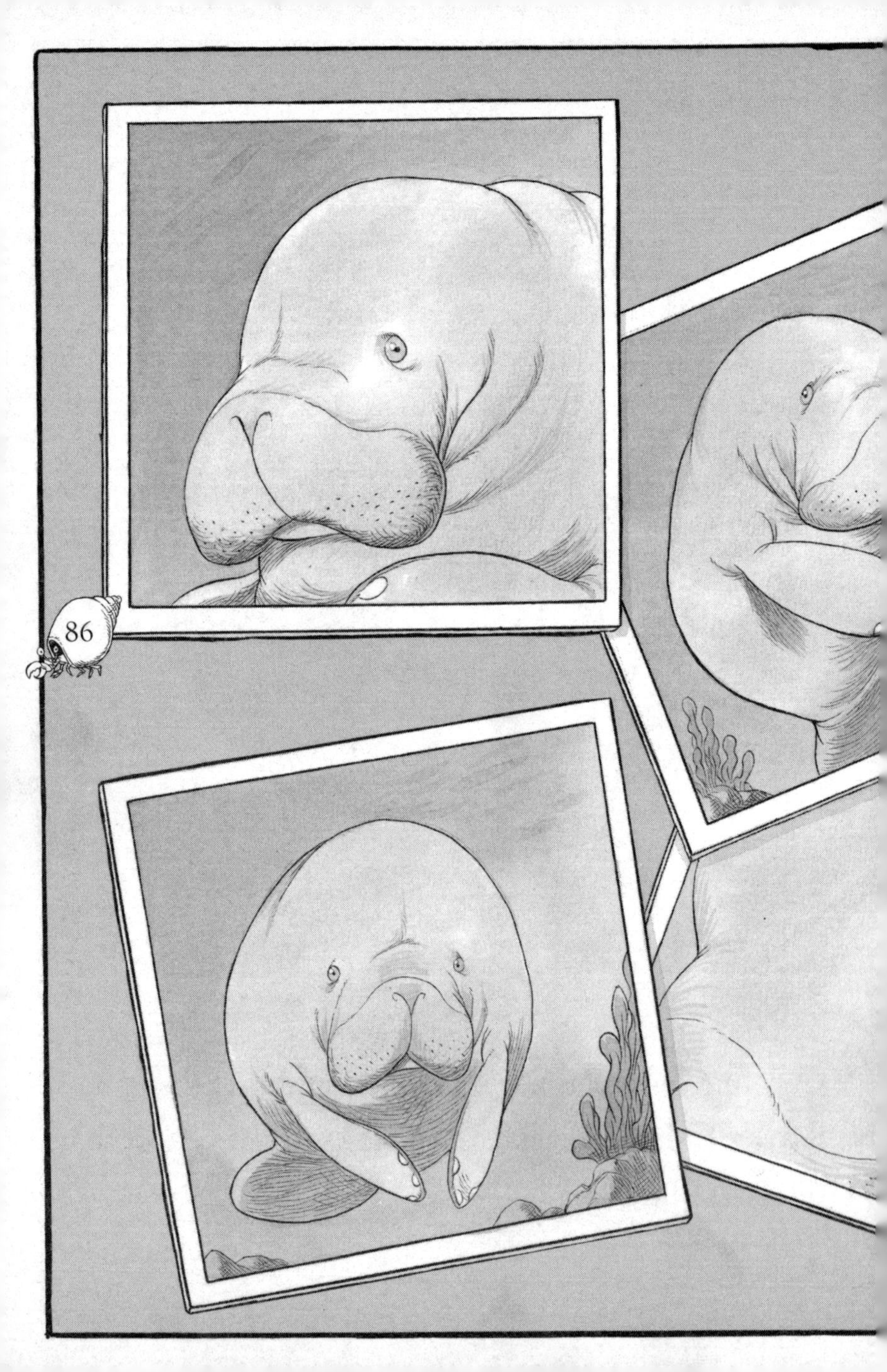

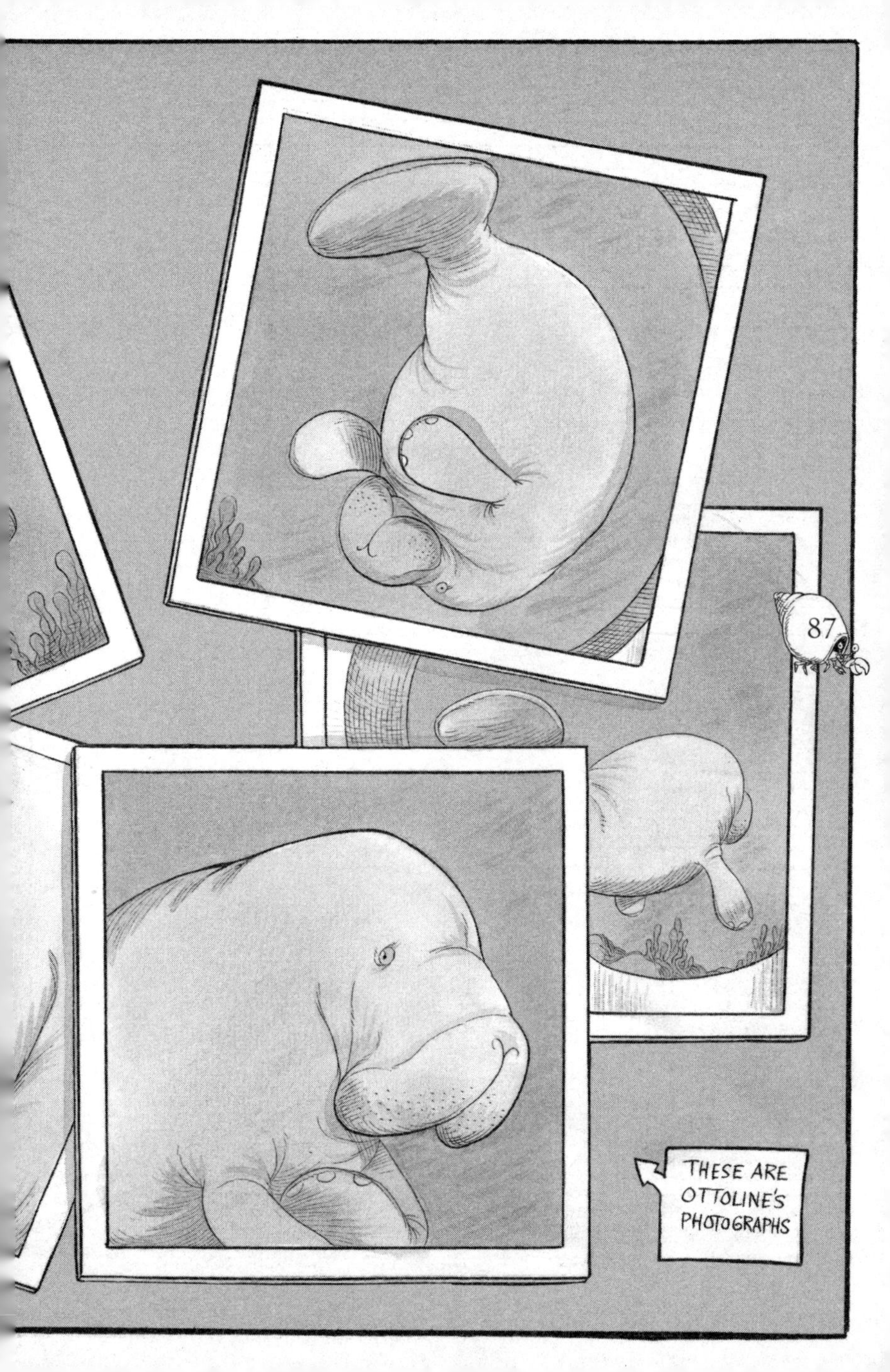
THESE ARE
OTTOLINE'S
PHOTOGRAPHS

Ottoline was busy sticking the photographs of the mermaid into her notebook when the bear came out of the captain's cabin.

"The captain's given me his second-best uniform coat," he said proudly. "What do you think?"

Ottoline smiled. "It suits you," she said.

Ottoline took her notebook to Captain Pasternak to show him her photographs.

Captain Pasternak was sitting at his desk, drawing pictures of imaginary mermaids.

"What have you got there?" he asked. Just then an alarm sounded.

"What's that?" said the bear. "Are we there yet?"

"I don't think so . . ." said Ottoline, looking out of a porthole.

"Nothing to worry about," said Captain Pasternak. "That's just the Iceberg Warning Alarm."

"Iceberg Warning Alarm?" said the bear.

"Yes," said Captain Pasternak cheerfully. "It warns you when you're about to hit a massive iceberg."

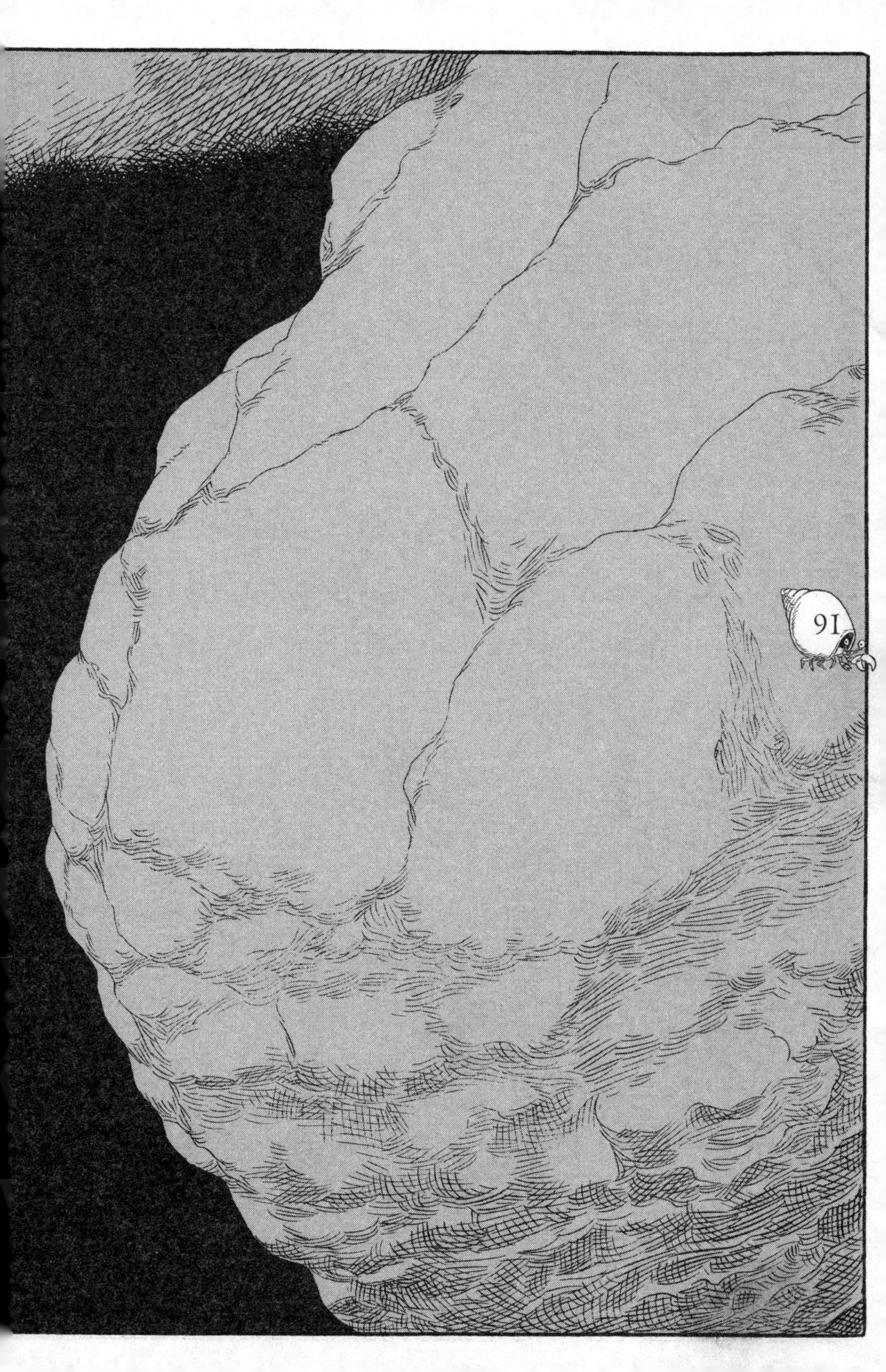

"Hold tight!" shouted Captain Pasternak, seizing the submarine's helm. "Crew, prepare to surface!"

Everyone slid to the stern of the submarine, except for Captain Pasternak, who was holding on tightly to the helm, and Nugent, who was swinging from the periscope.

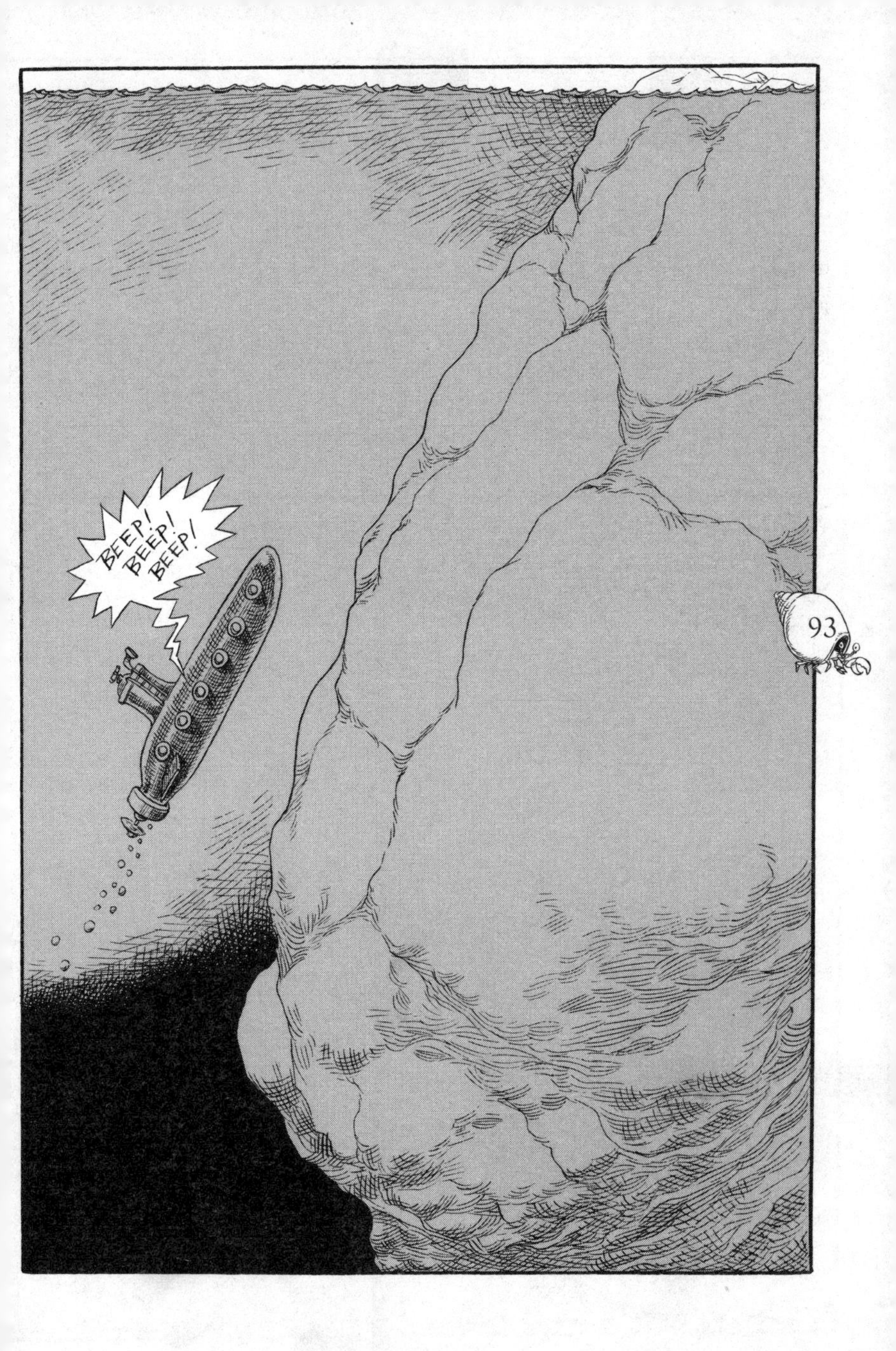
BEEP! BEEP! BEEP!

The *Iron Leviathan* surfaced just in time to avoid hitting the massive iceberg.

Captain Pasternak opened the hatch and everyone looked out.

"Hello," said some polar bears. "We were wondering when you'd show up."

Chapter Six

"Come inside," said one of the polar bears. "You're just in time for tea."

"Inside?" said Ottoline.

"Yes," said the polar bear, pointing towards the mouth of an icy cave. "This is just the tip of the iceberg."

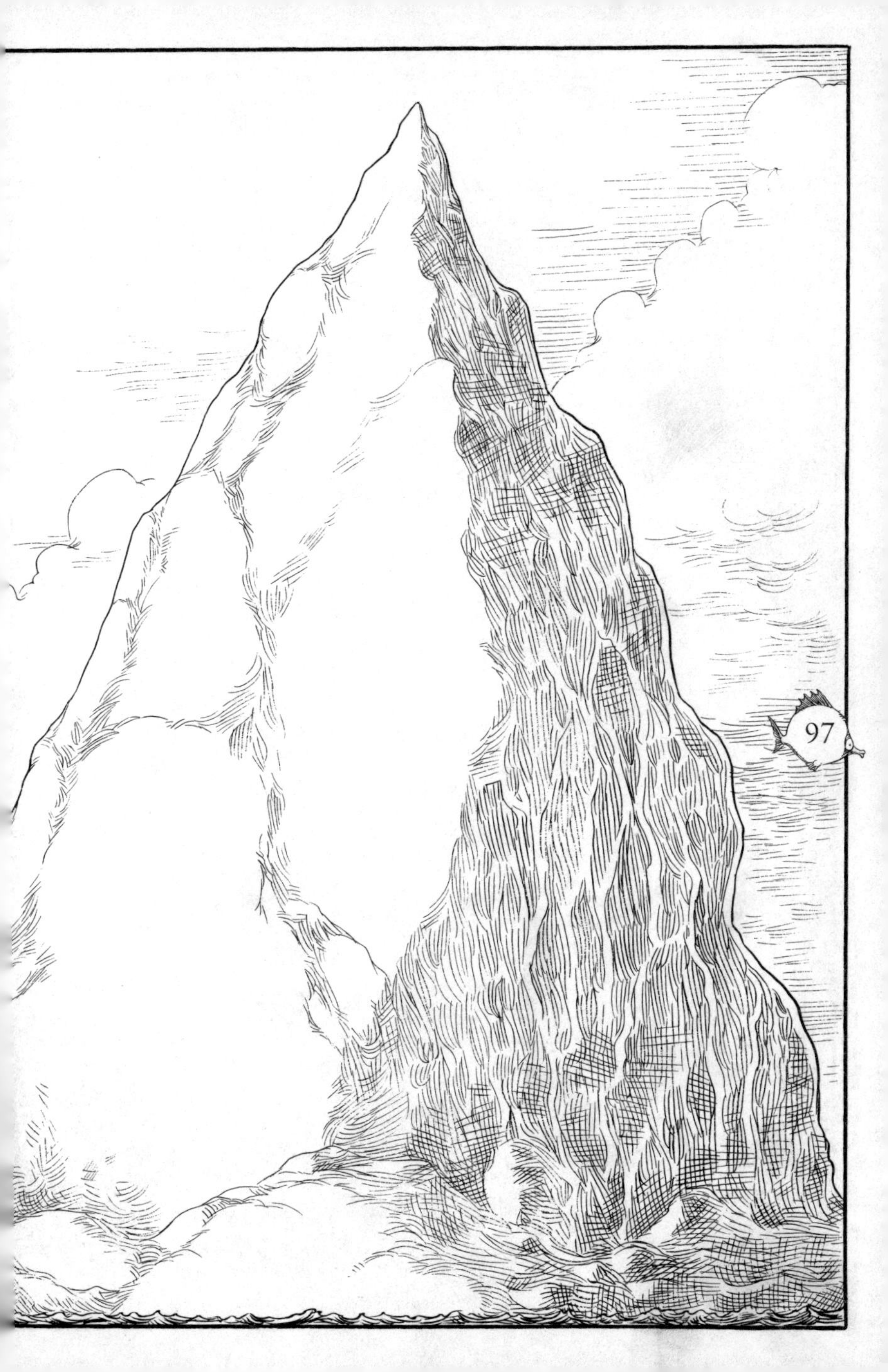

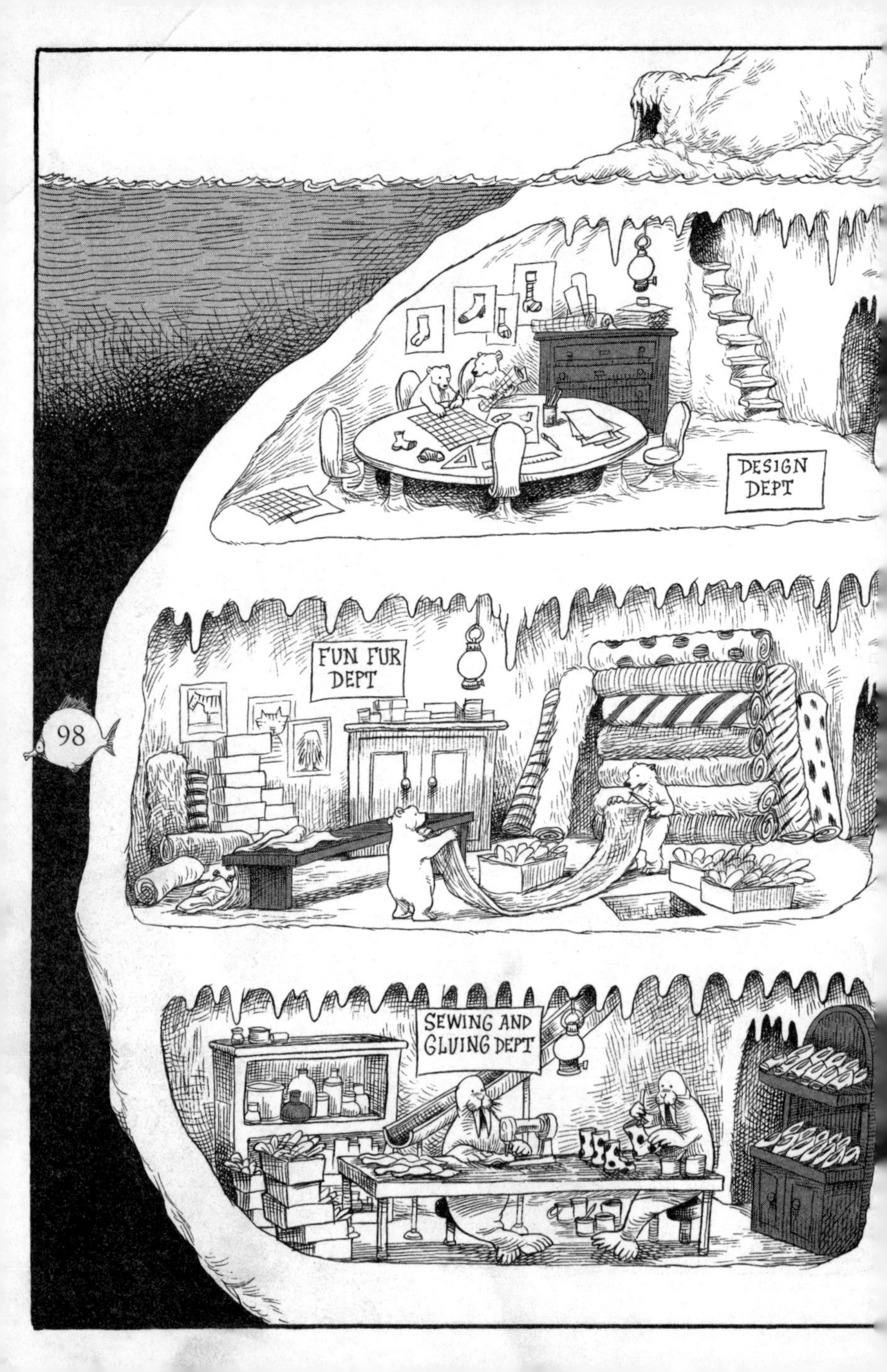
DESIGN DEPT
FUN FUR DEPT
SEWING AND GLUING DEPT

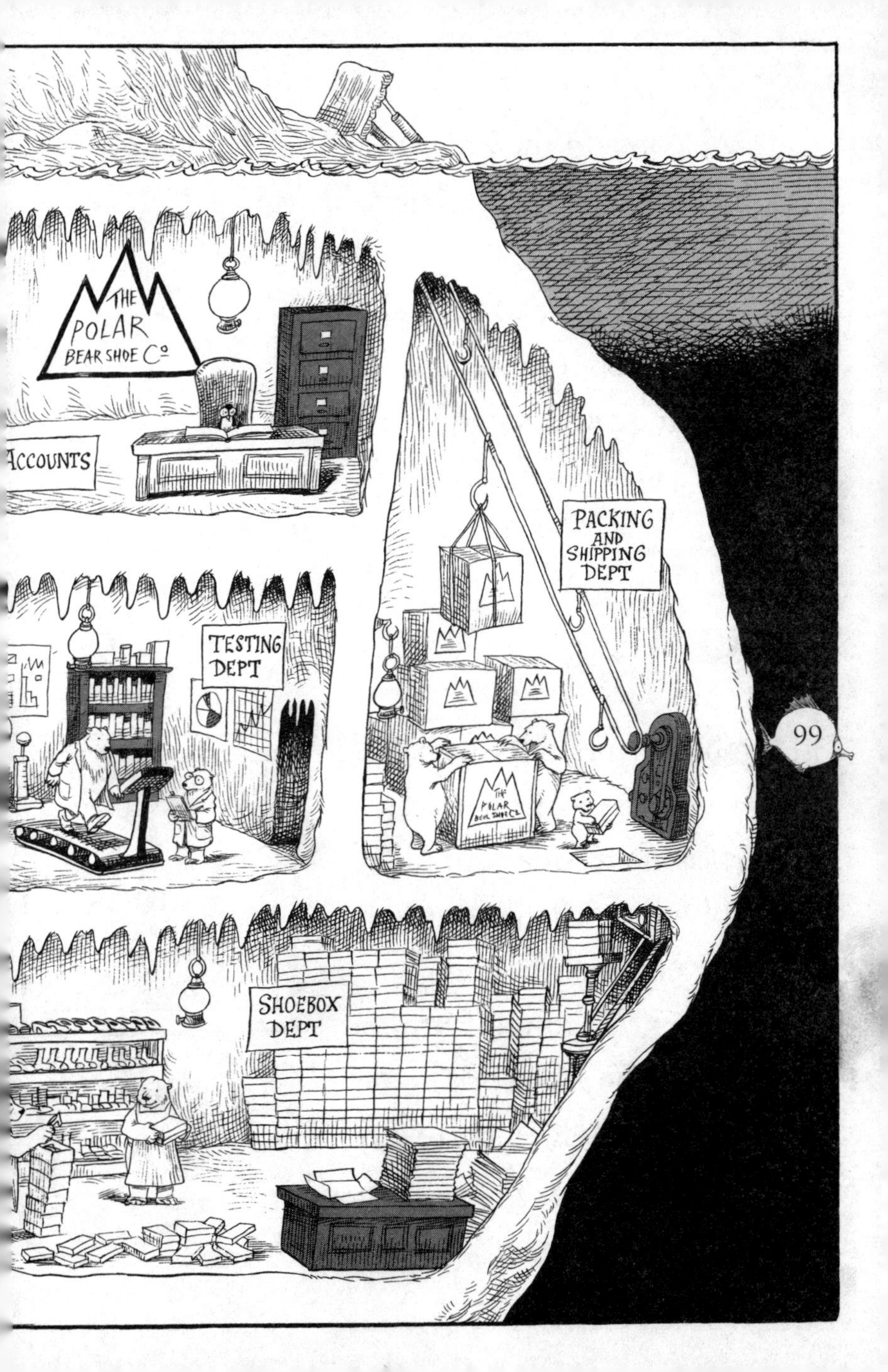
THE POLAR BEAR SHOE Co
ACCOUNTS
PACKING AND SHIPPING DEPT
TESTING DEPT
THE POLAR BEAR SHOE Co
SHOEBOX DEPT

"Welcome to the Polar Bear Shoe Company," said one of the polar bears. "My name's Libby."

"I have some of your shoes in my Odd Shoe collection!" Ottoline said excitedly. "I love your Penguin Slippers."

While Captain Pasternak and the crew of the *Iron Leviathan* unloaded supplies, Libby gave Ottoline and the bear a tour of the iceberg.

ANNE AND STEPHEN IN DESIGN

Stephen showed Ottoline a design he was working on. "It's called the Polar Choo-Choo Shoe."

Ottoline was very impressed.

Paul and Julie showed them some of their fun fur. "None of it comes from real animals," said Paul.

PAUL AND JULIE
IN FUN FUR

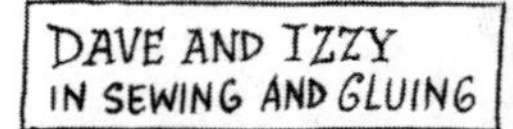

RICHARD AND URSULA
IN SHOEBOXES

Richard and Ursula worked in the Shoebox Department.

"I love shoeboxes," said Ottoline.

"Shoeboxes are my life," said Richard.

"Jeremy and Alice test all our shoes," said Libby. "For comfort, warmth and personality."

"Personality?" said the bear.

JEREMY AND ALICE IN TESTING

"You wouldn't want a shoe without personality," said Alice, ticking a box on her clipboard.

CONRAD, SARAH AND OSCAR IN PACKING AND SHIPPING

McNally worked in Accounts. McNally stared at Ottoline but didn't say anything.

MCNALLY IN ACCOUNTS

"Penguins have a natural talent for numbers," said Libby, "but they don't say much."

"Where are you travelling to?" asked Libby when they had finished the tour. The *Iron Leviathan* had been loaded with shoes for Big City and was ready to leave.

"Norway," said Ottoline.

"Land of Bogs and Beauty," said Libby thoughtfully. "Well, you'll certainly need a pair of these," she said, picking up a pair of enormous wellington boots.

"They're a little big for me," said Ottoline, "but I'll grow into them. Thank you very much."

Everybody from the Polar Bear Shoe Company came to the tip of the iceberg and waved goodbye.

"Thank you for the tea and the tour!" called Ottoline.

"We've got to get these shoes to Big City," said Captain Pasternak, "but I'm sure my good friend Minty Woodvine of the Arctic Mail will give you a lift."

Ottoline heard a droning sound and, looking up, saw a green seaplane in the sky above. It circled the *Iron Leviathan* three times and then came in to land on the water.

"THE TIN GOOSE"

S S TROND

111

Chapter Seven

"Ahoy there!" said the pilot of the seaplane. "Fancy flying into you, Captain Pasternak."

"This is Ottoline Brown and her assistant. They're on their way to Norway," the captain said.

"An Amateur Roving Collector, I see," said Minty Woodvine when Ottoline showed her her travel pass. "Well, this is your lucky day because Norway is on my route. Climb aboard."

"Thank you," said Ottoline, who was very impressed with Minty's long green hair.

"Fasten seat belts and prepare for take-off," said Minty Woodvine as she fired up the seaplane's engines.

"Goodbye, and thank you, Captain Pasternak," Ottoline called as the seaplane took to the skies.

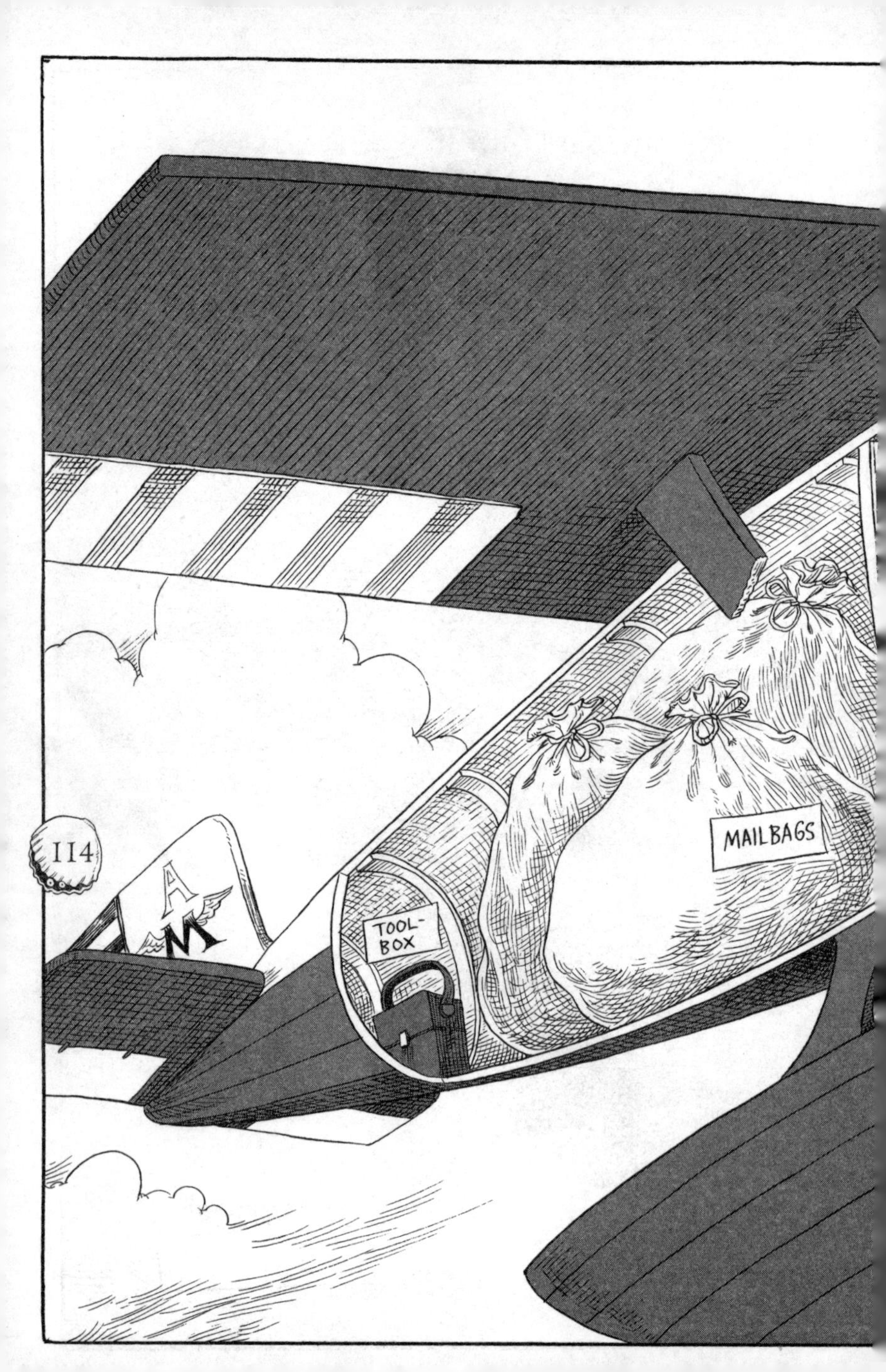
MAILBAGS
TOOL-BOX
A M

COCKPIT
ARMSTRONG-
SIDDLEY ENGINE
THE
TIN GOOSE

After a while the blue sky began to turn dark, and ominous-looking clouds began to gather around them . . .

. . . getting bigger and blacker the further they flew.

"It might get a little bumpy," said Minty cheerfully.

First of all it was a little bit bumpy . . .

. . . then it got very bumpy.

"So, why Norway, Land of Bogs and Beauty?" said Minty Woodvine brightly.

"I'm trying to find my best friend, Mr. Munroe," said Ottoline, trying not to look out of the window as the seaplane lurched to one side. "I think he's gone to Norway to help my parents look for Quite Big Foot—"

"The Abominable Troll of Trondheim?" said Minty in a shocked voice. "I hear it's eight feet tall, with claws like toasting forks and eyes as bright as headlamps and twice as scary! Why would anyone want to look for it?"

"Ma and Pa are Professional Roving Collectors," said Ottoline. "They're always on the lookout for interesting things."

"Well, I hope for their sakes they don't find it!" said Minty, shaking her head.

Just then there was a loud bang followed by a clunking sound.

"Hold tight!" shouted Minty. "Looks like we're in for a splash landing."

The seaplane swooped down out of the storm clouds towards the sea below.

Ottoline held on to the bear's paw and shut her eyes.

Everything went very, very quiet and then there was a tremendous . . .

SPL

SH!

Chapter Eight

Ottoline opened her eyes and looked out of the cabin window. The seaplane was bobbing about in the water next to a rocky island with a small wood on it.

Two green-nosed trolls came out
from the trees.

"I'm George and this is Ringo," said the first green-nosed troll.

"I'm Ringo and this is George," said the second.

"The flange bolt needs reflanging," said Minty, getting out her toolbox. "And the spatch lock needs unspatching. This might take some time . . ."

"Stay as long as you like," said George.

"This is a very small Norwegian wood, and we don't get many visitors," said Ringo. "Come inside for breakfast – we're having pancakes and herring."

THE NORWEGIAN WOOD
G
R
G
R
G
R

OTTOLINE'S NOTEBOOK
George
Ringo
(or maybe the
other way rou
gree
nos
Green-nosed trolls
Very good at
1. Cloud watching
2. Skimming stones
3. Fishing for herrings
Very bad at
1. Cooking herring
2. Making pancakes.
A Herring

Quite Big Foot

. 8 foot tall
2. Claws like toasting forks
3. Eyes like headlamps
4. Tangly hair
5. Snaggly teeth
6. TERRIFYING!

Later that afternoon, while Minty worked on the seaplane, the bear did some laundry and the green-nosed trolls skimmed stones, Ottoline sat down on a rock by the shore with her notebook.

She'd just finished drawing a sketch of Quite Big Foot when she looked up and saw a raft approaching. It looked very familiar.

"Thør Thørenssen, the famous explorer!" she exclaimed excitedly. "*The Whistle of the Wild – Tales of Animal Hitchhiking* is my favourite book!"

"Why, thank you," said Thør Thørenssen as he guided his Polynesian raft, the *Kon-Leeki*, in to land.

"Hello, Thør," said Minty Woodvine, joining them on the shore. She'd just reflanged the flange bolt and was taking a break before unspatching the spatch lock. "Ottoline and her assistant here are travelling to Norway. Can you give them a lift?" she asked.

"Certainly," said Thør, looking at Ottoline's Amateur Roving Collectors' travel pass. "All aboard!"

"My best friend, Mr. Munroe, has gone missing," Ottoline explained to Thør. "He's small and hairy and comes from a bog in Norway."

Thør Thørenssen stroked his yellow beard thoughtfully. "I think I might just be able to help," he said with a smile.

THE
KON-LEEKI

Chapter Nine

"I first perfected the Whistle of the Wild on my hot-air-balloon tour of the South Seas," said Thør Thørenssen as they sailed away, "when a passing albatross saved me from a volcano. Then, in South America, I met some very helpful llamas . . ."

"Yes!" said Ottoline. "You whistled and they carried you over the Andes. That's Mr. Munroe's favourite bit in your book." She sighed.

Thør put three fingers in his mouth and blew. Ottoline couldn't hear a thing, but the bear covered his ears.

"Ooo-wwwwww!" he yelped.

A few moments later two sea turtles surfaced next to the *Kon-Leeki,* followed by a large whale. Then a sea eagle appeared and dropped down on to the mast.

"Given a lift to anyone small and hairy recently?" asked Thør.

The turtles nodded, the eagle gave a screech and the whale blew water out of its blowhole.

"Can you show us where he went?" asked Ottoline.

The *Kon-Leeki* sliced through the waves until they came to the coast of Norway. Then they followed the creatures of the wild up a narrow fjord.

"My parents are looking for Quite Big Foot the Abominable Troll, and I think Mr. Munroe has gone to help them," said Ottoline. "He might be shy. But he's rather brave and quite helpful too. He—"

"Quite Big Foot!" exclaimed Thør, shaking his head, "Why he's . . ."

"I know," said Ottoline. "*Eight feet tall, snaggle-toothed and with a terrible temper and huge claws, sticking-up hair, eyes as big as headlamps . . .*"

"And quite big feet," added Thør. "At least, that's what they say."

At the end of the fjord Thør helped Ottoline and the bear ashore and gave a whistle.

The bear took a photograph of Ottoline standing with Thør Thørenssen.

"May I have your autograph too, please?" she said, blushing. "It's for Mr. Munroe. When I find him."

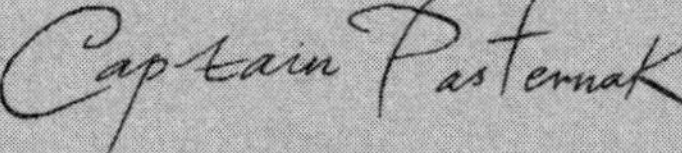

Minty Woodvine

OTTOLINE'S NOTEBOOK

Thør Thørenssen

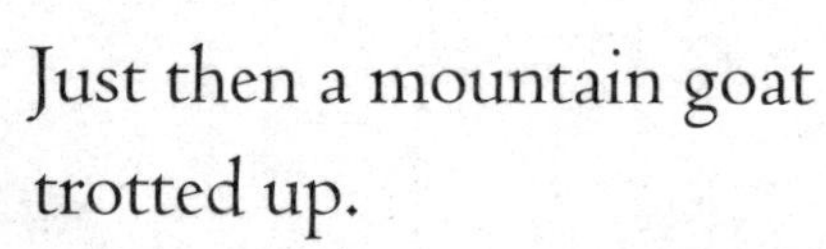

Just then a mountain goat trotted up.

"Ninian, at your service," he said. "How can I help?"

"Would you be so kind as to give my friends here a lift over the mountain to the bog on the other side?" asked Thør Thørenssen politely.

Ninian looked the bear up and down. "I'll need some help . . . Bradley!" he bellowed.

A large, shaggy Norwegian mountain ox came clip-clopping down the mountainside.

"Meet Bradley," said Ninian.

Thør waved goodbye. "Happy roving!" he called, readying the *Kon-Leeki* to set sail.

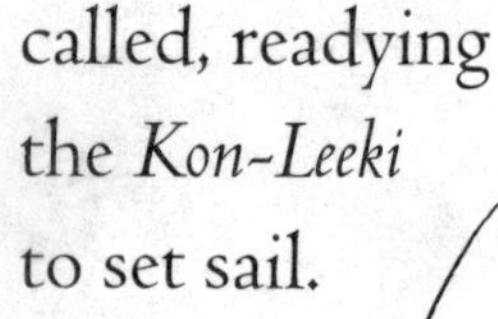

Chapter Ten

Ottoline, the bear, Ninian and Bradley travelled all the way to the top of the mountain. And all the way down the other side. When they got to the edge of the bog Ninian and Bradley stopped.

"Are you sure you want to go on?" asked Ninian. "It's cold and wet. And I've heard this is where Quite Big Foot the Abominable Troll lives. Apparently he's—"

"We know!" said Ottoline breezily. She turned to the bear. "Ready?"

"Ready," the bear said. He was shaking a bit but it didn't show under his Himalayan rainhood.

"Rather you than me," muttered Bradley.

Ottoline and the bear trudged through the bog. It was cold . . .

. . . and wet. Then it began to rain.

They didn't see anyone anywhere.

Then Ottoline heard a muffled sneeze. And then another. Following the sound, she came to a hole. In the bottom of the hole were two small, hairy Norwegian bog people.

"Good day," said Ottoline politely. "You haven't, by any chance, seen any Professional Roving Collectors passing through lately?"

The bog people shook their heads.

"What about a small, hairy bog person called Mr. Munroe?" she asked.

One of the bog people pointed.

Ottoline looked down and saw a trail of footprints.
"Mr. Munroe!" she gasped.

It continued to rain . . .

. . . heavily.

The footprints led into a deep, dark cave.
"I don't like caves," muttered the bear. "I much prefer basements and cupboards . . ."
"Follow me," whispered Ottoline.

QUITE BIG FOOT!

MR. MUNROE!

Ottoline stared at Quite Big Foot. He was huge and he did have quite big feet, but he wasn't scary at all. In fact, he looked rather shy.

"Are you the reason Mr. Munroe came to Norway ?" she asked.

Quite Big Foot nodded his shaggy head.

"But why didn't you tell me?" Ottoline said, turning to Mr. Munroe.

Mr. Munroe handed Ottoline the glasses he'd borrowed from Ottoline's parents' collection.

Ottoline put them on . . .

QUITE BIG FOOT'S CAVE
TRAVEL
SS TRONDHEIM

The

S.S. TRONDHEIM
BIG CITY ENQUIRER
TRAVEL
. . . and saw things more clearly.

"Oh, Mr. Munroe. I'm so sorry!"

Ottoline flung her arms around Mr. Munroe and hugged him tight. "I'll never ignore you again!"

"This cave reminds me of my cave in Canada," said the bear, looking around. "Cold and damp and miles away from anywhere – no wonder Quite Big Foot looks miserable.

"You should do what I did," he told Quite Big Foot, "and take a holiday."

"But don't you see? He *can't* go on holiday," said Ottoline. "That's the trouble. He's Quite Big Foot the Abominable Troll of Trondheim – troll spotters are out looking for him, telling stories about how big and fierce and scary he is . . ."

Quite Big Foot nodded his shaggy head sadly.

"They'll track him down," said Ottoline.

Quite Big Foot nodded.

"And point and stare and take photographs . . ." Ottoline went on.

A big tear ran down Quite Big Foot's hairy cheek.

"Unless . . ."

Ottoline smiled.

"You look fabulous," said the bear.

"Unrecognizable," said Ottoline.

Mr. Munroe nodded and Quite Big Foot smiled.

"I don't know how you do it, Ottoline," said the bear.

"Simple – with a little help from my friends," said Ottoline, "and a clever plan."

Back in Big City, Ottoline sat down on the Beidermeyer sofa with Mr. Munroe and kicked off her odd shoes. "You might come from a cold, wet bog in Norway," she said, "but I hope you know your home will always be here with me."

Mr. Munroe didn't say anything. He just shuffled a little bit closer to Ottoline and handed her the postcard that he'd found on the welcome mat.

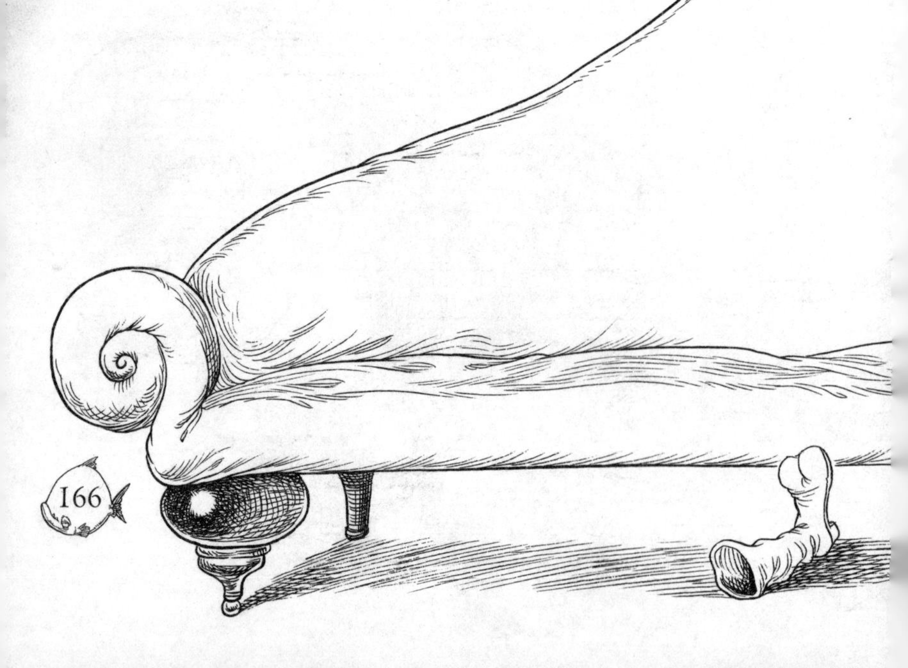

GREETINGS from the
SS TRONDHEIM
SS TRONDHEIM

Dearest O,

What a pity we missed each other in Norway! You're quite a roving collector now. Pa and I are very proud and think it's time you and Mr. Monroe joined us on a collecting trip. We are on our way home,

lots of love,

Ma.

P.S. We never did find Quite Big Foot!

P.P.S. Don't forget to put the bog goggles back.

Miss O. Brown,

Apartment 243,

The Pepperpot Bld.,

3rd Street,

BIG CITY,

3001

First published 2010 by Macmillan Children's Books

This edition published 2015 by Macmillan Children's Books
an imprint of Pan Macmillan
a division of Macmillan Publishers Limited
20 New Wharf Road, London N1 9RR
Associated companies throughout the world
www.panmacmillan.com

ISBN: 978-0-330-47201-2

Printed and bound by CPI Group (UK) Ltd, Croydon CR0 4YY
1 3 5 7 9 8 6 4 2